Growing Readers
New Hanover County Public Library
DISCARDED
from
New Hanover County Public Library
Purchased with
New Hanover County Partnership for Children
and Smart Start Funds

GIGANTIC!

HOW BIG WERE THE DINOSAURS?

PATRICK O'BRIEN

HENRY HOLT AND COMPANY ♦ NEW YORK

STEGOSAURUS

"ROOFED LIZARD"

This lumbering leaf eater had
a brain the size of a meatball.

ANKYLOSAURUS

"FUSED LIZARD"

This enormous armored brute was a walking tank.

ELASMOSAURUS

"THIN-PLATED LIZARD"

This massive sea monster
swam through ancient oceans
on giant flapping flippers.

SPINOSAURUS

"SPINED LIZARD"

This bizarre beast had a
six-foot sail on its back.

QUETZALCOATLUS

"FEATHERED SERPENT"

This flying giant soared above the
dinosaurs on long, leathery wings.

PHOBOSUCHUS

"FEARSOME CROCODILE"

This monstrous reptile swallowed animals whole.

BRACHIOSAURUS

"ARM LIZARD"

This towering behemoth's extra-long neck held its head four stories above the Jurassic plains.

TRICERATOPS

"THREE-HORNED FACE"

This mighty giant's massive head
was a dangerous weapon.

SEISMOSAURUS

"EARTH-SHAKING LIZARD"

The supergiant Seismosaurus shook
the earth with its tremendous weight.

DINICHTHYS

"TERRIBLE FISH"

This colossal underwater killer
terrorized ancient sea creatures.

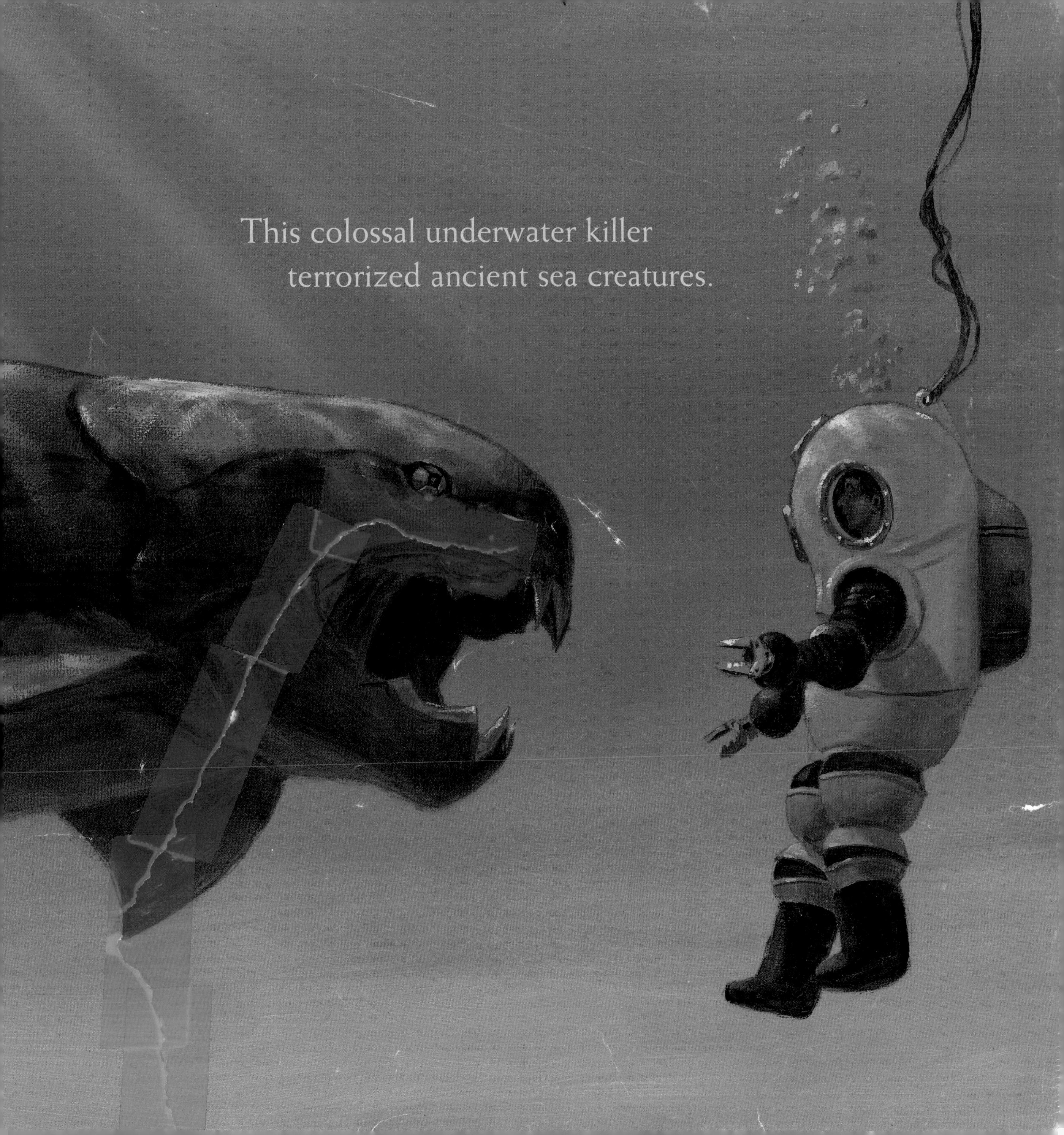

PARASAUROLOPHUS

"SIMILAR-RIDGED LIZARD"

This peaceful plant eater
used its head as a trumpet.

TYRANNOSAURUS REX

"TYRANT LIZARD KING"

This king-size killer ruled
the beasts of ancient America.

GIGANOTOSAURUS

"GIANT SOUTHERN LIZARD"

This terrifying monster
was even bigger than T. rex.

COMPSOGNATHUS

"DELICATE JAW"

In a world of gigantic beasts, this diminutive dinosaur—
the smallest of them all—just tried to stay out of the way.

◆ **STEGOSAURUS** (STEG-o-SAWR-us) was about 30 feet long and weighed about two tons. It had huge spikes on the end of its tail. These spikes were good for fighting off a big meat eater looking for a big meal.

◆ **ANKYLOSAURUS** (ang-KYL-o-SAWR-us) was 35 feet long and as wide as two trucks parked side by side. It had thick, bony armor on its back and head, as well as a heavy club made of bone on the end of its tail. These features gave it good protection against hungry tyrannosaurs.

◆ **ELASMOSAURUS** (ee-LAZ-mo-SAWR-us) was about 46 feet long. It was not a dinosaur but a huge marine reptile. It lived in the sea but still had to come up for air, just as whales and dolphins do today. Also, Elasmosaurus may have dragged itself up onto land to lay its eggs, just like a modern sea turtle.

◆ **SPINOSAURUS** (SPY-no-SAWR-us) was a huge creature. At about 49 feet long, it was even longer than T. rex, but not as heavy and strong. Its backbone had tall spikes sticking up from it, which were covered with a "sail" made of scaly skin. No one is quite sure why Spinosaurus had such an odd feature.

◆ **QUETZALCOATLUS** (KET-sol-ko-OT-lus) was not a dinosaur. It was a pterosaur (TAYR-o-sawr), a flying reptile. With a wingspan of about 50 feet, this was by far the largest flying animal ever on Earth. Its giant wings were made of tough skin stretched between its body and its very long pinky bones.

◆ **PHOBOSUCHUS** (foh-bo-SOOK-us) was related to the crocodiles we have today, but it was a lot bigger. It was about 40 feet long and had a six-foot-long skull. It probably lurked in the shallow waters of swamps, waiting patiently. A dinosaur that came too close would be suddenly snatched up in its enormous jaws.

◆ **BRACHIOSAURUS** (BRAK-ee-o-SAWR-us) may have been the tallest dinosaur. Its head was about 45 feet above the ground. Like an oversize giraffe, Brachiosaurus could eat leaves from the tops of trees that most other animals could not reach.

◆ **TRICERATOPS** (try-SAYR-ah-tops) was about 30 feet long. The three large horns on the front of its head allowed Triceratops to do battle with the largest predators around, even tyrannosaurs. Triceratops also had a strong shield made of solid bone on the back of its head for extra protection.

◆ **SEISMOSAURUS** (SIZE-mo-SAWR-us) was one of the heaviest dinosaurs ever. It probably weighed about 100 tons—as much as fifteen large elephants. It was the longest dinosaur yet discovered—about 150 feet long. That's as long as half a football field.

◆ **DINICHTHYS** (dye-NIK-theez), sometimes referred to as Dunkleosteous (dun-KEL-os-tee-us), was probably 20 to 30 feet long. It was a great big fish with a big bony head. The whole front part of its body was completely encased in thick bone. Its teeth were not real teeth; they were sharp, pointed skull bones. Even its eyeballs were protected by a ring of bones.

◆ **PARASAUROLOPHUS** (PAR-ah-sawr-OL-o-fus) was about 33 feet long. It had a six-foot-long crest on the top of its head. Inside the crest were hollow tubes that connected to the animal's nostrils. This allowed Parasaurolophus to make loud honking noises by blowing through its nose.

◆ **TYRANNOSAURUS REX** (tye-RAN-o-SAWR-us REKS) was about 45 feet long and probably weighed about eight tons. It was a gigantic beast, but its arms were very small. That didn't matter, though, because its huge jaws and six-inch fangs did most of the work.

◆ **GIGANOTOSAURUS** (JEE-gan-o-to-SAWR-us) was discovered in 1995 in South America. It was about 50 feet long and weighed about seven tons. That's the biggest meat eater we know about—so far.

◆ **COMPSOGNATHUS** (komp-SOG-nath-us) was only two to four feet long, including its tail. It was a fast, agile little dinosaur, with small sharp teeth. One Compsognathus fossil was found with its last meal still undigested in its belly: a small lizard that apparently wasn't as fast as Compsognathus.

AUTHOR'S NOTE

The word "dinosaur" comes from the Greek words *deinos*, meaning "terrible," and *sauros*, meaning "lizard." This name was invented in the 1800s. In those days, dinosaurs were poorly understood because very few bones had been found. Scientists thought that they were giant ancient lizards. We now know that is not true. Dinosaurs were reptiles, but they were not lizards.

It is not easy to know exactly how big dinosaurs were. Scientists decide what a dinosaur looked like, and how big it was, by studying its bones. But complete dinosaur skeletons are very rare. The bones are usually found broken and scattered. Dinosaur skeletons standing in museums are put together like a giant puzzle. Bones from different animals of the same species are used, and missing pieces are added by sculptors. The length of one of these mounted skeletons is not necessarily the actual length of the living dinosaur.

Scientists know that any species of dinosaur would have included millions of individuals. Yet for most of the species we have found only a few skeletons. This makes it difficult to determine the average size of a dinosaur. For instance, only one Giganotosaurus skeleton has ever been found. Perhaps it was the biggest one of its species that ever lived. Or perhaps it was the smallest! We may never know for sure.

For Allison, as always

Special thanks to Dr. Cameron Tsujita, Department of Earth Sciences
at the University of Western Ontario.

Henry Holt and Company, LLC, *Publishers since 1866*
115 West 18th Street, New York, New York 10011

Published in Canada by Fitzhenry & Whiteside Ltd.,
195 Allstate Parkway, Markham, Ontario L3R 4T8.

Library of Congress Cataloging-in-Publication Data
O'Brien, Patrick. Gigantic: how big were the dinosaurs? / by Patrick O'Brien.
Summary: Explains the names of fourteen dinosaurs, from Stegosaurus to Compsognathus, and describes their physical characteristics, size, and probable behavior. 1. Dinosaurs—Size—Juvenile literature. [1. Dinosaurs.] I. Title.
QE862.D5027 1999 567.9—dc21 98-26038

ISBN 0-8050-5738-2 / First Edition—1999 / Typography by Meredith Baldwin
Printed in Hong Kong
10 9 8 7 6 5 4 3 2
The artist used oil paints on canvas to create the illustrations for this book.